I0531505

TOXIC TRUTH

BROTHERHOOD PROTECTORS WORLD

TINA DONAHUE

Twisted Page Press LLC

TOXIC TRUTH

Only he stands between her and a hired killer.

When Kenzie discovered a toxic truth that harms military personnel, the international corporation where she worked put a hit on her. Desperate to survive, she escapes to the Crazy Mountains to hide out at a deserted cabin she recalls from childhood.

Lucas owns the property now. As a former Ranger and sniper, he's never met a more terrified young woman. Yet despite her fear, she's determined to bring her former employer to justice.

Not without his help.

Fearless, honorable, and sexy as sin, he's the hero she's always needed.

There's no turning back as they surrender to their mounting passion for each other and meet danger head on to bring a criminal enterprise to justice, saving those service members most at risk.

ACKNOWLEDGMENTS

A special thanks to Elle James for inviting me to write for her Brotherhood Protectors series. I love her characters and those of the other talented authors who are expanding this wonderful world.

Also, thanks to Kate Richards' Wizards in Publishing and editor Laura Garland for her insightful edits. And to Nicole Austin for another beautiful cover.

BROTHERHOOD PROTECTORS

ORIGINAL SERIES BY ELLE JAMES

Brotherhood Protectors Series

Montana SEAL (#1)

Bride Protector SEAL (#2)

Montana D-Force (#3)

Cowboy D-Force (#4)

Montana Ranger (#5)

Montana Dog Soldier (#6)

Montana SEAL Daddy (#7)

Montana Ranger's Wedding Vow (#8)

Montana SEAL Undercover Daddy (#9)

Cape Cod SEAL Rescue (#10)

Montana SEAL Friendly Fire (#11)

Montana SEAL's Mail-Order Bride (#12)

SEAL Justice (#13)

Ranger Creed (#14)

Delta Force Rescue (#15)

Montana Rescue (Sleeper SEAL)

Hot SEAL Salty Dog (SEALs in Paradise)

Hot SEAL Hawaiian Nights (SEALs in Paradise)

CHAPTER 1

CRAZY MOUNTAINS, Montana

"MOVE, DAMMIT!" Kenzie Caltrane pounded her steering wheel and rammed her foot against the gas pedal. "*Go.*"

Her back tires squealed in place, kicking up mud and digging her deeper.

Shit, shit, shit. This can't be happening.

If the company goons caught up to her now…

Silencers on their guns would muffle any noise, tonight's rain washing away her blood, the Crazy Mountains' rural locale perfect for them to bury her where no one would look or find as much as a bone.

Her stomach cramped. Tears stung her eyes.

For fuck's sake, she was a pharmaceutical engineer, not a CIA spy. She'd only wanted to stop a horrible outcome for—

Something flashed in her peripheral vision. Headlights? *Noooo.*

They couldn't have gotten here this quickly. She'd turned off her damn lights and had driven close to blind for miles, which sent her veering into this depression.

Panicked, she popped her door and scrambled outside.

Wind battered her, rain speckled her glasses, and her loafers sank into the gooey earth. Stifling a frustrated cry, she backed away from her vehicle into the murky darkness, whatever she'd seen before gone.

Yet still out there. Danger pressing close. Worse, they could hear her damn motor.

Rather than running blindly into the trees, she climbed back into her car and shut it off.

Other than wind whipping around her vehicle and rain pinging on its roof, the silence out here was complete.

She fought for a full breath but couldn't manage one.

Escaping to the middle of nowhere hadn't been as smart as she'd thought.

What now, what now, what—

Something approached from the woods, the shape dim but huge.

A damn bear?

She'd read about hungry grizzlies breaking into vehicles for something to eat. Unwilling to be a sitting target should the thing attack, she bolted from the car and stumbled away. Mud sucked at her shoes, slowing her down. Fighting it, she slogged in the opposite direction for a tree to hide behind.

The thing lumbered toward her.

Her foot hit an obstruction. *Oh.* Pitched backward, she flailed her arms and fell against a trunk, a low-hanging branch snapping against her. Searing pain shot down her neck to her shoulder. Teeth clamped, she whimpered.

Loud breathing sounded. Not hers.

She froze.

A horse, rather than a bear, clopped forward until its rider reined it in. A dark slicker covered the man's forehead, shadows obscuring his face.

Her pulse jumped. All night she'd dodged unknown vehicles, hoping none would catch up. To have her killer arrive this way didn't make sense but wasn't something she'd question.

She sidled around the tree.

He dismounted. His height next to the horse put him at six-three or more, his shoulders broad. He regarded her car off to the side.

Leave. Check it out.

The second he reached it and looked inside, she'd tear through the forest as well as she could.

He faced her, weird glasses on his eyes.

Night vision goggles.

Her heart slammed into her throat. If his equipment detected a thermal signature, she hadn't a chance to escape detection.

She snatched back her hand and hid it within her jacket, hoping he hadn't seen anything.

He and the horse stepped closer.

Sucking air, she withdrew an equal distance from him and stepped on something.

Snap.

She flinched.

His horse made a funny noise.

"Easy." He rubbed its neck, his attention never leaving where she hid. "Hey. Do you need help?"

His resonant voice boomed in the relative quiet, proving his youth. Early thirties, she guessed, and more trouble than she needed. No way would she make a sound to bring him closer. Feeling sick, she pressed her lips together.

He lowered his head then lifted it. "I know you're out here. I saw you and your car." He shouted, "Do. You. Need. Help?"

Despite the cold air, heat prickled her face, fear and indecision making her sweat. If he were with the others and trying to trick her into revealing herself, his voice would clue them into where she'd stopped. If not, he'd unknowingly help them and might possibly get murdered in the process.

"Look, I'm trying to—"

"*Quiet.*" She stepped from behind the tree. "Don't shout."

As he took her in from top to bottom, his

hood bobbed up and down. "Why?" He leaned to the side and regarded the surroundings then pulled a rifle from a holster tied to his saddle. "Did you see an animal?"

Facing one seemed less daunting than this. Outrunning a mountain lion or bear held some hope, a bullet none. She trembled uncontrollably. "Yeahhhh." Fear she couldn't fight sounded in her voice. *Damn.* "Over there." She pointed away from her.

He looked.

She ran. Rocks stubbed her toes. Mud pulled off her right shoe. Crying, she cursed both.

"What are you doing?" He caught up and grabbed her arm.

A shriek tore from her. She pummeled his chest. "Let go! Don't hurt me!"

"Hurt you? I'm trying to help."

She twisted her arm, releasing herself. "Like hell." She lurched back. "My friends know I'm here. I called them a few minutes ago. They live at the top of the road. They have guns, too. They're coming to get me."

"Yeah?" He rubbed his chest where she'd hit him. "That's damn remarkable, considering *I* live where you're saying, which means your friends don't. Since *I* don't have smartphone reception down here, you couldn't. Why won't you let me help you? Your car's stuck. You're obviously lost and soaked. At least let me do something about that."

She hugged herself but couldn't stop shivering, her lightweight jacket not keeping the rain or wind out. "Something as in what, exactly?"

"I have a waterproof blanket, all right? It's yours if you want it."

"Back at your place, you mean." She shook her head. Raindrops wiggled down her lenses, making him and the surroundings wavy. "No thanks."

"The blanket's in my saddlebag. Once you have it, you can stay here if you want while I go back to my cabin and call for help."

"Wait." He hadn't moved, but she couldn't risk it. "Help?" She pulled sodden hair off her face. "You mean 9-1-1?"

"I was thinking along the lines of a garage to tow your car out. No need to bother emergency services with that."

What he said sounded reasonable, but taking a chance on him telling the truth could prove deadly. Her skin grew clammier. "Why are you wearing night vision goggles?"

His eyebrows inched up. "So I can see?"

She didn't appreciate his sarcasm. "Yeah, I know that. But why? And why are you out here at night in the rain? What were you looking for?"

"You."

Hell. She fell to her knees and grabbed the largest rock she could find then lifted it to her shoulder, ready to hurl the damn thing at him. "Don't come any closer."

Wind pushed his slicker aside. Rain dampened his worn jeans. "If I wanted to hurt you, I could have well before now when I first arrived." He lifted his rifle.

Her stomach fell. "Put it down. *Now.*"

"No problem." He lowered it to his side, the muzzle pointed at the ground. "To answer your questions, when you were gunning your motor—I presume to get out of the mud—the wind carried the sound to my place. I don't often hear cars up here, especially stuck ones, so I came out to investigate and to help. If you'd let me." He shoved his rifle back into its holster, unbuckled his saddlebag, and pulled out the blanket. "If I hand this to you, will you promise not to clobber me with the rock?"

Amusement sounded in his strong voice. Not the mean kind, but teasing, as a man does when he's flirting.

Yeah, right. Out here in the dark and rain, them alone, except for the thugs following her.

She pushed to her feet. "How far can you see with your goggles?"

"Why?" He stepped closer. "Are you expecting someone?"

Unwilling to say, she gripped the rock harder. "Answer me."

"If you're asking if they're also binoculars, they are. Meaning I can see damn far. Why do you want to know?"

"Did you see anything besides me and my car when you were coming down from your place?"

He muttered something beneath his breath.

"What?"

"No, I didn't see anyone else, all right?" He held the blanket to his chest. "You and I are alone here."

Whether that was good or bad, she didn't

want to know. "Take off your goggles, binoculars, whatever they are. They're creepy."

"They're… Never mind. Anything to keep you happy." He pulled back his hood and removed the things.

His hair was dark, eyes a light color she couldn't determine. Even in the scant light, his features were masculine as fuck and hotter than sin.

Her heart turned over. If she'd seen him in a bar or at a social gathering, she would have drooled in appreciation. Out here, she wanted more proof he was a good guy and not a paid killer who enjoyed his work. "Who are you? Why do you live here? If you do."

"*If* I do?" He laughed, the sound deep and rich. "Do you honestly think I spend my evenings riding in rain for fun? Trust me, I don't. Who are you, and why are you out here in this weather?"

Telling him the truth wasn't happening. He'd either dismiss her concerns as ludicrous or might think she was a nutcase and would call in authorities she couldn't trust. "No matter what you claim, my friends *are* here." Whether he'd believe her lie or not, she didn't care. He'd never get the truth from her. "There's a mountain resort they're staying at. I pulled off the road to check my directions and got stuck in the mud. That's it."

"Hardly."

"There's nothing else, dammit."

"Except you're freezing." He unfurled the blanket and wrapped it around her. "Better?"

His lime scent comforted rather than alarmed. His concern brought tears to her eyes. Unable to trust her voice, she nodded and dropped the rock.

"Thanks for that." He gestured to it. "Now, about the story you just told me. Your car doesn't have GPS to tell you which way to go? If it does have that, you figured it was wrong so you wanted to check directions on your smartphone even though there's no reception here? Look, you need to tell me why you're really at this spot for me to help you as I'd like."

"I *was* heading for a resort."

"Not around here. The only one in this vicinity doesn't exist any longer."

She already knew as much. It closed a few years back, making it the perfect hideout. "I own the property. I wanted to get away for a while and intended to use it."

"You're referring to Elk Resort?"

Lying wasn't possible this time. He was a local and would know if she named a place he didn't recognize. "Yeah."

"Then you're wrong again." He eased the blanket closer to her throat. "I own the resort, all one-hundred-and-eighty acres and what used to be ten cabins. There's only one left now, where I live. Since you weren't coming to see me, why are you out here when you're clearly not dressed for it?"

She spoke through her teeth. "It's a free country."

"So I've heard." He glanced past her then retrieved her shoe. "Want me to help you put this on?"

"No." She yanked it from him and pushed her muddy foot inside. *Gawd.* Slime would have felt better. "Who are you? You never answered me."

"You mean, besides the property owner here? Name's Lucas Rome. This is Caesar." He stroked the horse's mane, which was as dark as its body and his hair. "Your turn."

She couldn't chance him knowing who she was if his buddies were looking for her. It didn't seem likely, given his easy-going personality and what he'd already revealed about himself. However, risking anything at this point wasn't wise. "Why is my name important?"

"Are you a movie star or some kind of internet sensation?" He worked his mouth to stop his smile. "Afraid I'll recognize you from your name rather than how you look at this point?"

A drowned dog probably had her beat in the beauty department. Hardly caring, she rubbed the blanket over her lenses to dry them but left thick smears instead.

"This might work better." He pulled a rag from his back pocket. "It's clean."

After taking it, she worked on her glasses, uncertain whether to feel bad for treating him like a criminal or to maintain her caution as to what he might do next. Vigilance won out. "Anything else you can tell me about yourself?" She pushed the rag in her jacket pocket. "Like why you're up here alone— You are alone, right?"

He scratched his stubbled cheek. "If you're asking if I have a wife and kids, it's a firm no on both counts. There's no long-term girl-friend in my cabin either. How about you? You running from an ex-husband, ex-lover, or a current one in those two categories?"

"Why are you in the middle of nowhere?"

New muttering beneath his breath. "Because I like it?"

She swore.

"Easy." He used the same voice on her that he had with Caesar.

For some reason, it didn't piss her off but made her tired instead. "I can't tell you how much it'd help if you gave me some details as to who you are."

Understanding and kindness rose in his eyes. "Fair enough. I'm former military, Army." He lifted his slicker. Beneath it, he wore a Ranger sweatshirt. "When I left the service, I came home to Montana. Had a chance to get this property and took it."

That didn't make sense. "You're so rich you bought this place and don't have to work any longer?"

He grinned, his smile wide and inviting.

"Don't I wish, but no. Even if I had the funds, I'd still want to keep busy and offer my assistance to anyone who needs it. I'm in security, so to speak. I work on assignment. When each ends, I return here to wait for my next call."

Sincerity rang in his voice and showed on his luscious face. More importantly, he wanted to help people. Still… She'd been cautious for so long, her misgiving lingered. "What did you mean by 'so to speak'. It's either security or it's not. Which is it?"

"Do you always ask so many questions?"

She bounced in place. "I don't know you."

"Hey, I gave you my blanket, I've offered to call for help to get your car out, and I don't know you either. Not even your name. Is it a secret?"

She looked to the side. "Kenzie Caltrane."

"Was that so hard?"

His softened tone and big body called to her as few things had. She was fucking weary and scared, and simply wanted to melt into his arms and beg him to make things better. Which he couldn't. One man who worked security didn't have that power. Damn, getting involved in her problems might get him killed, too. "You shouldn't have stopped to help."

"Why not?"

"Because you *can't*." The tears she'd held back for weeks poured out, turning into hitching sobs. "You'll get *hurt*."

"Hey, hey." He gathered her to him in a protective caress. "Nothing's that bad. No one's that powerful. If your current or ex, or whatever, is after you, I can get you to a safe place and—"

"You *can't* stop the entire government." She pushed away. "You *can't* stop an assassin."

His features slackened. "What?"

She put out her hand, warning him to keep his distance. "Go back to your cabin. Pretend you never saw me. Forget my damn name." A new sob caught in her throat. "You *can't* help."

"Calm down, please." He lifted his hands but didn't touch her. "I'm not going anywhere. I sure as hell don't intend to leave you out here alone to face whatever—"

"You. Have. To." She edged back. "There's no choice. If you think you can call 9-1-1 and fix this, it isn't possible. The federal government is involved. They'll bury you."

Alarm sparked in his eyes then faded, resolve replacing it. "Involved in what? What are you talking about? Who are you?"

For once, she got in his face. "I'm a toxic truth to the feds and others. They don't want me around. That's why they've put a hit out on me."

CHAPTER 2

DURING HIS TIME with the Brotherhood Protectors, Lucas had worked several unique assignments, though none as strange as what Kenzie just said. Nor had he ever seen a young woman as terrified and defeated, yet gutsy enough to keep fighting.

Despite him outweighing her by seventy pounds or better and being a head taller, she shook her fist at him. "Go away."

Not in this life, and definitely not until she was safe. Having her dry, warm, and a smile lighting up her pretty features was his first goal...as soon as he learned every detail as to what they faced. Particularly who was stalking her and their proximity to his cabin.

First though, he needed her to settle and trust him. "You asked earlier what I meant by 'so to speak.' When I said security, I didn't mean being a mall cop or babysitting a business to make sure only the right people get inside. I work for Brotherhood Protectors. Everyone involved is former military—Rangers and snipers, like me, Delta Forces, and SEALs. Hank Patterson, the guy who started the group, is a former SEAL. Our cases involve ordinary people, those at the very top of the food chain, and everyone in between. We've seen and done it all. We *can* help you. Beginning now."

"No, you—"

"Shut up and listen to me." He gripped her shoulders. "I need you to be straight in answering my questions. Why are you at this particular locale? Do you know someone on the adjacent properties?"

She pushed her cat-eye glasses up her nose, her hand shaking. "My parents used to come to Elk Resort when I was a kid. I remembered it. After reading about it closing, I thought I could hide out here."

You will with me. He'd accept nothing less. "Where did you drive from?"

She named the city. "New Solutions Pharmaceuticals, also known as NSP, is headquartered there."

The pieces began to fall into place. "You worked there and found out something you shouldn't?"

"That's putting it mildly." Her mouth trembled. "I'm a pharmaceutical engineer."

Not an occupation he would have guessed given her appearance. She seemed so young, mid-twenties or a little older, at most. He released her. "You told your superiors what you discovered?"

"I had to." She flapped her hands. "The project I was working on was for the armed forces. Military personnel you probably know. NSP products are supposed to keep them in combat condition longer than ever. Instead, they're hurting and killing them, no matter what the CEO says."

Jesus. During his tours, he'd learned about pharmaceuticals meant to keep personnel alert or to treat various ailments, including PTSD. He rubbed his mouth. "Did you see anyone following you tonight?"

"I thought I did. That's why I was driving

without lights, which made me run off the road."

"Come on." He took her hand.

"Wait." She tried to break free.

He wouldn't allow it. "We need to go back to your car so I can check it for a tracking device. No matter how far you run, if they know where you are, they'll catch up."

She moaned then struggled to match his pace.

The vehicle's undercarriage proved clear, as did the trunk and interior. He popped the hood. No device there either. Maybe she'd imagined someone following her or overreacted to the problem she faced. Over the years, Big Pharma and the feds couldn't hide all their dirty laundry, but putting a hit out on a civilian, a scientist for Chrissake, seemed extreme.

"Did you find anything in there?" She peered at the engine.

Her flowery scent wafted toward him, making his cock stiffen and his balls ache. Her guileless look and the trust in her light-brown eyes made him want to hug her from here to tomorrow and promise nothing bad would ever happen. "No. Are you absolutely sure someone was—"

"*Yes.*" She bared her teeth. "I'm not crazy or on drugs. Every turn I took, this black van followed. Not too close and not too far. Just enough to keep me in sight."

"How'd you lose it?"

She pushed back her auburn hair. "I had my signal on for a right. When the light turned green, I took a hard left, cutting in front of oncoming cars. One almost hit me. Until I was a few miles from here, no one followed. Then headlamps popped up in my rearview mirror. In this location. In this freaking weather." She gripped the lip of the car. "That's when I shut off my lights and took several detours. Eventually, those behind me disappeared. Before you showed up, I thought I saw something glinting in the distance."

Without a tracking system, whoever had tailed her wouldn't have caught up...if she was remembering events correctly. Panic screwed with people's brains, making them believe things that hadn't happened. "Who besides your supervisor at NSP knows what you've discovered?"

"The CEO and his board. I didn't bother with my department head. I took my concerns directly to the top."

"What happened?"

"The SOBs said I'd falsified records then fired me. I contacted the feds next, as a whistleblower. When they did nothing, I threatened to go to the press. That's when the threats started." She shuddered. "At first, it was late-night phone calls. Then anonymous text and email messages. The last one came in this afternoon, very short and sweet. It said, 'Drop your lies or you're dead before the day ends.' Believing them, I ran."

He cursed himself for his earlier doubt. "Does anyone know your parents used to come to this resort? Will those at NSP contact your mom and—"

"They died when I was a child. I'm alone. No one knows about my connection to this place except childhood friends I haven't seen in a decade or more."

If nothing else, assassins were thorough in researching their targets' backgrounds. However, there was a faster and surer way for them to locate her. "Take off the blanket."

"What?" She held it closer to her throat, her teeth chattering loud enough to draw Caesar's attention. "Why?"

"To check if you're wearing a tracker."

"Huh?" She rounded the car, putting it between him and herself. "How could I? I would have noticed."

"Not if they used the tiniest one available, which I'm guessing they did."

"That's nuts." She dug her nails into the blanket. "How could anyone have gotten it in my clothes?"

"Do you frequently wear the jacket you have on?" He approached slowly to avoid spooking her. "In the last few days, has anyone bumped into or brushed up against you?"

Her mouth opened and closed. She bent over the back fender. "Oh my god."

He took that as a yes and pulled the blanket from her then felt her jacket collar. No device there. "Don't move."

A statue couldn't have stood as still.

Both pockets proved empty, except for the rag he'd given her. Next, he checked the hem. On the right side, where she'd never notice, he fingered something hard. He guessed not a spare button, the item rectangular not circular. To confirm his suspicions, he pulled his knife from its sheath on his belt.

"Holy hell." She skittered back.

He followed and used his calmest tone. "I need to open the lining on your jacket. That's all. Is it okay with you?"

Chewing her lip, she stared at the blade, but nodded.

Finished, he held the tracking device in his palm.

She clutched her throat. "How did it get in there?"

"My guess is, while you were out, someone broke into your place and put these in several clothes you've been known to wear on a frequent basis. They likely played it safe to make sure they could constantly track you. Did you bring any extra jeans, jackets, or shirts along tonight?"

"No. Nothing. Only what I have on."

"I need to see your shoes." He gestured for them.

For once, she didn't ask anything and willingly handed both over. No device inside. "I have to check your jeans now and your top, unless you'd rather do it."

"I'll do my sweatshirt and you can do my jeans. Up to my knees, no farther."

They worked as a team and discovered nothing else. He lifted the device. "Now to get rid of this."

"Throw it as far as you can from the car. If they don't see my vehicle, they may think I didn't get to this spot."

They already knew where she'd been, and that she'd stopped. Their only question was why she'd done so. "I have a better idea."

He slipped it into his front pocket, tugged her to Caesar's side, then laced his fingers, palms up. "Put your foot in the center of my hands. When I push up, swing your other leg over Caesar."

The way she regarded the saddle, the thing might as well have been a torture device. "I don't know how to ride a horse."

"You don't have to. I'll guide him from behind you. He's as gentle as a puppy. Bullet's another story."

"Bullet?"

"My dog. Mean mother. He'll rip out

anyone's throat on my command, including whoever's been following you. No more questions." He shook his hands. "Your foot here. Now."

The moment she'd plopped on the saddle, she grabbed the horn for dear life. Each breath she panted out fogged the air.

"Cover your mouth." He showed her how. "Otherwise, you might faint, and I'll have trouble hanging on to you."

She sneered.

He lowered his face to hide his smile. How he could find humor at a time like this wouldn't have made sense to the average person. Being former military, he understood what danger did to a person. During operations, he and his buddies would crack dumb jokes then dissolve into hysterical laughter. Facing death wasn't doable without some levity to break the tension. Somehow, ribbing each other made everyone feel invincible even though they understood how foolish that thinking was.

Seated behind, he wrapped the blanket around her shoulders then rested his arm on her waist. "I have you." Liking her weight and warmth against him, he touched his cheek to her hair. "Try to relax."

She grasped his arm. "Please tell me we're not riding back to your cabin."

That would be dumb. "We're going in the opposite direction. This might take a while."

"Why?" She dug her nails into his hand.

A little extra pressure and she'd draw blood. He tensed to keep from complaining. "I swear everything is all right and will stay that way."

"Where are we going?"

"The best place to get rid of the device."

"Such as?" She broke her death grip on him then twisted to see his face. "An abandoned mine shaft?"

Always a good choice, except there weren't any around here. "The ones I know about are too far. Your glasses…" They hung lopsided on her nose. He straightened them, surprised at how cute they looked on her. "Better?"

She blinked rapidly then squinted. "Except for your thumbprint on the lens."

Try to be nice… "Jeezus priest, woman, you are fucking hard to please."

Her mouth shook. Rather than cry, she nodded. "I am, aren't I?"

Warmth flooded him at her gentle admission, doing miraculous things to his nuts and dick, preparing them for some serious action.

Like that's going to happen. They were escaping hired killers, not enjoying a date.

"Sorry." She searched his eyes. "I'm kind of unglued, you know?"

He did.

"I'll try to be less demanding, okay?"

"Promises, promises." He arched one eyebrow then winked.

Smiling softly, she settled against him, calmed as he'd wanted.

They rode in silence, nothing except pattering rain, whistling wind, and Caesar's occasional snorts intruding upon the peace. Pine and other vegetation scented the air, creating a wondrous fragrance and an altogether nice experience.

Despite the numerous women he'd dated, he'd never shared a moment like this with them. There'd been booze to drink, dancing to enjoy, concerts, rodeos, and other events to indulge in, always followed by sex until he and the women in question couldn't think, breathe, or move.

He tightened his hold on Kenzie.

She looked over her shoulder at him.

Before she could ask anything he didn't want to answer, he lied, "The path's bumpy here. Don't want you jostling around if Caesar's footing gets dicey." A lame excuse, but the best he could offer on the fly.

"If that's the case, shouldn't we walk so Caesar doesn't have the extra weight to carry?" She squeezed his hand. "I don't want him hurting his legs."

"He won't. But thanks for worrying about him."

"Always. He's a good boy. Aren't you, Caesar?"

To Lucas's surprise, she leaned forward, pressed her cheek to Caesar's mane, and stroked the long hairs. "You're quite the handsome stud, aren't you?"

He tried hard to sound serious. "Uh, he's a gelding."

"Oh no." She lightly smacked Lucas's thigh. "Why'd you do that to him?"

For obvious reasons. "I couldn't have him running off to every mare in heat. Have you ever tried to control a stallion that has one thing on its mind?"

"No need to paint a picture." She straightened and turned her face to his, their mouths inches apart. "I trust you've made up for what he's lost?"

Rain dripped over her plump bottom lip, inviting him to lick off each bead. At least, until she slugged him, which was her right. He took a deep breath and blew it out. "What?"

"You love him, don't you?"

"More than you can imagine. Bullet, too. If anyone tried to kill them… I'd die to protect both."

Dread filled her eyes. "You shouldn't be helping me. I don't want you or your fur babies getting hurt."

Fur what? "Believe me, they won't. Caesar would bolt, Bullet would attack, and I'd fire my weapons. You do recall me telling you I was a sniper, right?"

She curled her upper lip. "I get that you had to do what was necessary in the service, but you're out now. I don't want you murdering anyone on my behalf."

Before this was over, she might think

differently. "If it's self-defense, it's not murder. Your safety comes first."

"Our safety." She squeezed his wrist. "I won't have it any other way."

"You really have no idea how this works, do you?"

Rain ran into her eye. She lifted her glasses and wiped it away. "I know how I am, and I'm not going to be different because I'm in danger. We both matter. Arguing your points won't change how I feel."

Fuck, you're something. Brave, obstinate, and foolish came to mind. She must have been a handful at the lab where she worked. *Good for you.* His admiration for her increased a thousandfold, which made liking her too easy. Others he'd protected had worried about themselves to the exclusion of everyone else, even loved ones at times. While their ass was in danger, they couldn't consider anyone else.

During her earlier meltdown, he'd believed she was like them. Not even close. She'd rightfully worried about his intentions. Hell, he'd come out of nowhere, carried a rifle, and was a stranger. Worse, a man. Some guys, when alone with a woman out here, would have easily taken advantage and blessed their good luck. "I never argue when I have no chance of winning."

"Glad we're on the same page."

"Afraid not." He wheeled Caesar in a new direction. "I'm not crazy, which means I'd never put myself in harm's way for the hell of it. I will protect you though, whether you want me to or not, no matter what. It's what I fucking do."

"I don't care if that's what—"

"This isn't up for debate. I can't change your mind or stop what you believe, and it's impossible for you to do either with me. Let's leave it at that and get through this as best we can, all right?"

"No, it's not." She released his hand.

He missed her softness and heat instantly.

"If it comes down to my survival or yours, I'll let them take me." She lowered her face. "It's only right. This isn't your battle."

Frustration tensed his shoulders. If he could have bellowed without drawing attention to them, he would have. "You can't sacrifice yourself for me. You don't fucking know me."

"So, what? Do you know the people you put

your life on the line for? Is each a friend or relative?"

He tugged his hood farther down his forehead. "This is different for me. It's my job."

"This is my belief. Same difference. We shouldn't talk any longer." She turned away from him.

Fuck. Their first fight and they barely knew each other.

Unwilling to goad her into another argument she wouldn't let him win, he kept his peace. Just as well. Rushing water sounded in the distance.

She stiffened. "Is that a motor?"

"A creek."

Arriving at it, Lucas reined Caesar in and dismounted.

Kenzie reached for him. "Where are you going?"

"To the bank." He pulled the tracking device from his pocket. "To get rid of this."

"What if it's not waterproof? The signal will stop, and they'll come to my car."

"The feds don't mess around with their equipment. This baby isn't what average folks can buy on the market. That's sissy stuff. I'd wager this thing will hold up in the creek or anywhere else that's wet."

He pitched it into the cascading water that ran downstream for miles, leading her assassins far away in their pursuit to harm her.

CHAPTER 3

An open area showcased Lucas's cabin, towering pines and firs nestled nearby, a mountain range rising majestically behind them, the air crisp and rain-scrubbed.

If Kenzie had arrived here before seeing him, she wouldn't have asked why he chose to live in this place. Its natural beauty astounded, the seclusion a definite plus. The only drawback was the cabin's floor-to-ceiling windows, plus lights burning inside showing every-damn-thing.

Her stomach rolled. "Do you have drapes or blinds in there?"

After helping her dismount, he regarded his place. "Never needed them. No one's around." He touched her hand. "They won't be."

His confidence soothed better than she would have predicted. She hoped hers would eventually catch up.

A growl sounded.

She flinched and pressed close to him. "What was that?"

"Nothing to worry about. Bullet. *Quiet.*"

The largest and blackest German shepherd she'd ever seen rose to its feet and padded from the shadow it had hidden in toward the top step on the porch. Where it thankfully stayed. "Do you like black animals for a reason?"

"I do. No one can see Caesar or Bullet coming in the dark."

A wise choice.

He tended Caesar in a small shelter to the left. Rifle poised at his side, he then led her to the front door.

Bullet watched her closely.

"Put out your hand." Lucas bumped her shoulder. "Let him sniff you."

Easier said than done, given his size. Trembling, she did as requested.

The shepherd's gentle nudging and cold,

wet nose broke her tension. "Aw, that's a good baby." On her knees, she scratched behind his ears. His panting slowed and sounded curiously similar to a human's sighs. She laughed. "You're a good boy, aren't you?"

"The best." Lucas opened the door. "How about we go inside? Get you dry and warmed up."

Except for countless windows, this place couldn't have been more inviting from its arched ceiling to the rustic décor, heavy on leather and other masculine furnishings. Its scrupulous cleanliness surprised her. So did the appetizing roasted meat, onion, and garlic scents.

Her stomach rumbled.

He eyed her. "When did you last eat?"

"Yesterday." The never-ending threats had killed her appetite.

"That won't do." He removed his boots near the door, put his rifle on a side table, and hung up his slicker. "By the time you've showered and dried off, I'll have dinner reheated."

She clutched the blanket to her throat. If the tracking device failed, they might need to escape quickly. Being naked during that wasn't her dream scenario. "I'm good."

"You're muddy."

Her loafers had dirtied his shiny floor. Even Bullet, who rested near the leather sofa, hadn't left any paw prints. "Where's your mop? I'll clean up the mess I made."

"Not as my guest, you won't." He pulled the blanket from her. "The shoes and socks go on the mat next to my boots. You can hang your jacket by my slicker."

She did as he'd suggested then used his rag to blot her face and clean her hands.

"Back in a sec." He returned holding several large towels, something hanging from his pocket. "So you're a Stanford grad."

Her sweatshirt bore the name. "That's me."

"Smarter than hell, huh?"

I wish. "Not in what counts. I should have gone to the press first, rather than the company and the feds."

"I don't know about that." He pulled thick socks from his front pocket. "These will warm up your toes."

"I couldn't."

"Relax. They're clean."

That wasn't something she would have doubted. Seated on a side chair, she pulled them on, the tops reaching close to her knees they were so large. "Did the military teach you to be neat?"

"Among other things." He scrubbed his face and hair dry. A leather cord fell to the floor, his black, shoulder-length locks dangling free, making him look like a pirate. Big and imposing but not dangerous, decency in his beautiful green eyes.

Her pussy creamed, and her nipples peaked to a painful point. She'd never been around such a gorgeous or gracious man. Those in school were uniformly nerdy and treated her as if she were a moron, barely able to draw in a breath without direction, much less competent enough to compete against them. Graduating first in her class hadn't changed their opinions or impressed the men she eventually worked with. Their attitudes toward women in her field were as juvenile.

Lucas tossed his towel on another chair. "What makes you think the press would have believed what you discovered about the meds?"

It took a moment before his question registered. "Hard data." She stood and used the rag to swipe the seat clean. "I copied everything without the department head knowing what I did." She reached inside her bra and pulled out three flash drives.

His eyebrows rose. "Good move on hiding them there. I would never have guessed."

She snickered. "I wasn't going to put them in a purse, that's for sure."

"Mind if I show what you have to Hank?"

The name didn't connect at first, then she recalled what he'd said earlier. "Your boss."

"And friend." He pulled a platter from atop the fridge and a pot from inside, the living room flowing freely into the dining area and kitchen. "While the stew and biscuits heat up, I'd planned to call him." He turned on the oven and a burner. "What do you like to drink?" He leaned against the counter, ankles crossed.

The prominent bulge behind his fly captured her full attention. Her mouth went dry. She forced herself to glance away. "Uh…"

"I have beer if you need to relax."

She would have preferred hard liquor and sleeping within his arms for a month, except that crazy dream wasn't going to happen. "Do you have hot chocolate?"

"Coming up." He pulled the box from a cabinet.

"Let me." She put her flash drives on the table and joined him at the stove. "While I fix our meal, you can call Hank." She grabbed the box.

He didn't let go, their fingers touching, his lime scent and natural musk surrounding her.

Aroused and dizzy, she locked her knees to keep from sagging against him.

"Like I said, guests don't work in my place." He leaned down to her. "Calling Hank can wait until I feed you. No one's going to show up tonight."

The magic between them vanished, her insides rolling. "You can't know that for sure. I don't want you or your babies getting hurt."

A tender smile tugged at his rich mouth. "They won't, and I sure as hell won't let anything happen to you or me. Relax, please." He eased a stray tress off her cheek.

In a fair and sane world, she would have kissed his palm then begged him to hold her, which he'd gladly do. After enjoying their meal and playing in bed, they'd cling to each other, sated and content.

God, I'm hopeless. Before she lost all good sense, she pulled the box free and shooed him away. "Call your boss. Let me work in peace."

"You don't know where everything is."

"I'll figure it out. I'm smart." She touched the Stanford logo. "Not blind."

He shook his head and washed his hands. "Have it your way."

While she cleaned up then found bowls, plates, and utensils, he brought a laptop to the table and a landline phone.

"Are you using a phone because it's more secure than Skype?"

"Not exactly." He powered up his computer. "I wasn't sure you wanted Hank seeing you." He slung his arm over the chairback and took her in as he had outside. "Not that you don't look amazing, but I didn't want to spook you."

Already, he knew her too well. "I like keeping the lowest profile available."

"Which you'll do here, believe me. Only I'll know your deepest, darkest secrets." He offered a sly grin. "And I'm not telling."

She laughed, the good, deep kind that

relaxed and refreshed. "Bad boy." She wagged the wooden spoon at him. "You need to take lessons from your babies."

"You're sure about that?" He stroked the chair lightly and teasingly, as he might a woman's nipples.

Hers tightened.

"You like your men docile?"

Not him, not ever. In bed, she'd want him unleashed, asking nothing, taking everything because she'd already agreed. Him on top or beneath her, in front, and behind, his cock filling each opening, his weighty and warm balls tapping her ass and then her chin when she went down on him. "I doubt even hand-cuffs and a blindfold would make you that way."

His eyes rounded. "You're into that stuff?"

Heat burned her face and throat. "I was trying to illustrate my point, not speaking literally."

"Uh-huh."

She shouldn't have liked his teasing, but did. "Your call to Hank?"

"Right." Rather than lift the receiver, he

fingered the flash drives. "Shouldn't I download these first?"

"You could try, but they're password protected and encrypted."

He whistled. "Damn, you don't fool around. You're amazing, know that?"

Hell yeah, she did. Belief in her abilities was the only thing that got her through school and work. Still, his praise and approving smile quickened her pulse. She liked both far better than him complimenting her on silly stuff like looks. "Thanks." She took a slight bow.

"You should be opening this data while I get dinner." He stood.

She pushed him back down. "Call Hank. Put him on speaker." It wasn't that she didn't trust Lucas, but expecting him to remember and relate everything his boss said wasn't something she wanted. "Please."

"Will do." He patted her hand and punched in a number.

Each unanswered ring made her heart jump.

Click. "Hey." Hank's voice wasn't as deep as Lucas's but still impressed. "It's late. What's up?"

"Kenzie Caltrane. A woman who needs our help."

On the other end, rattling and a female voice sounded in the background, then tapping sounds, like someone keying into a computer. "Give me the details."

"I need a towing service at my property pronto to remove her car. Here are the coordinates."

She forgot to stir the stew, not understanding how Lucas could know latitude and longitude without a compass. He hadn't used one when they'd been outside.

The clicking stopped. "She crashed?"

"No. The vehicle's stuck in the mud. We need it away from here and hidden ASAP."

She tapped Lucas's shoulder. "Tell him about the hit out on me."

Hank's voice poured from the speaker, "The what?"

"Hit." She leaned toward the phone. "The feds or the pharmaceutical firm I used to work for, possibly both, have a contract out on me. There was a tracker in my jacket. Lucas tossed it in the creek. It's supposed to be waterproof, but we all know manufacturers lie about their products, especially those with government contracts. If it's stopped transmitting, goons are going to show up here, guns drawn. You have to help him. He can't get hurt. Neither can his babies."

Hank cleared his throat. "Him who? What babies?"

Lucas gestured her to silence then spoke to Hank. "Give me a sec." He pulled her back to the stove. "Don't budge from this spot." He'd lowered his voice so only she could hear. "I mean it. Take a step toward the phone and I'll have Bullet guard you. He won't be licking your hand this time. If I tell him to bare his teeth at you, he will. He follows my orders, not yours."

She crossed her arms. "I was only trying to tell Hank what happened since you're taking forever to do so."

"There's a method to my madness." The oven pinged. "Stay here. Make sure the stew doesn't burn, and don't forget to put the biscuits inside this thing"—he rapped the stove —"rather than leaving them on top."

And here she'd thought he was close to perfect. In a pinch, men always condescended to women to get their way. "Maybe you should write out your directions so I don't forget."

"Only when I have time." He chucked her chin. "For now, stay…please."

His request did it. So did his playful touch. "Sure."

Back on the call, he explained her concern for his safety, along with Caesar and Bullet's, aka his babies.

Hank made a muffled sound. Could have been laughter. "Got it. While you were…occupied a few seconds ago, I dispatched a crew to take care of the vehicle. We'll store it in one of our facilities. Their ETA should be less than an hour."

"How about a perimeter guard?"

"A what?" She closed the oven door. "You mean men guarding this location so no one gets close?"

Lucas nodded.

Hank spoke, "I'll have men stationed on every road leading to your place. Your security system's still operable, right?"

"It is." Keying into his computer, he brought up several outside images: the front porch, backyard, the cabin on each side, and the kitchen showing him at the table, her shifting from foot to foot by the stove. "Everything's up and running."

She gripped his chair. "What if someone shoots out the cameras?"

He lifted his face to hers, his features serene. "They'd have to find them first."

"Yeah, I know." She dug her nails into the wood. "Aren't there devices to do that?"

"There are, but I've already taken precautions against them."

The truth? A lie to make her feel better? "Please be straight with me."

He pushed out a breath. "The lenses aren't at eye level where someone could detect them easily. They're at a height no one would expect. If by some chance a device could, and anyone shoots them out, an alarm sounds. It's loud enough to wake the dead in every county in this state. I've also booby trapped the areas around the cameras."

She realized something. "You saw me on your system after you heard my car."

He nodded.

Backing away, she pointed at him. "I could have gotten hurt by one of your traps."

"Only if you'd messed with a camera."

This is nuts. "Is someone after you, too?"

"No," Hank said. "At times, we've needed a secure location for our clients, and we've used Lucas's cabin, given its isolation and security. Trust me, you couldn't be in a better place or in finer hands. He'll take great care of you."

Lucas's face flushed, darkening his olive complexion, but he didn't look away from her.

Something inside her fluttered, the walls she'd built around herself beginning to crumble. Hardly a wise choice, but she couldn't stop her feelings for him. "I agree with your assessment, Hank. Can I call you that?"

He chuckled. "Of course. We're family here."

They had Lucas's back and hers despite them not being blood. She couldn't have been happier for him. He deserved Hank, his other military buddies, and every good thing life offered. "Thanks. About payment for this…"

"We'll discuss that later. For now, we need to focus on Lucas keeping you and his babies safe."

Lucas rubbed his eyes. "How about we get on with this?"

There's more? Already strung out, she wasn't eager to hear it and spoke to him, her voice lowered. "While you do, I'd like to clean the mud off."

"Give us a minute, Hank." He frowned at the entryway then her. "Not happening." He spoke softly. "Remember me telling you that?"

"I meant here." She pointed at her soiled jeans. "I'm ready to take you up on your earlier offer."

Confusion then understanding filled his face. "The bathroom's down there." He gestured to the lone hall. "Everything you need is inside."

Except something fresh to wear. She fingered her sweatshirt. "I didn't bring along extra clothes."

"You can have mine." He gestured her away. "I've got plenty that are newly laundered. I'll put them on the bed."

Mouthing "thank you," she then gave him a thumbs-up and retreated alone to the bathroom, wishing he were beside her.

CHAPTER 4

THE MOMENT the bathroom door closed, Lucas took the phone off speaker and made certain to keep his voice down. "This is fucking serious, Hank." He told him about the meds fucking up the soldiers' health.

Hank swore. "Did she tell you how?"

"We hadn't gotten that far yet. Hold on." He shut off the burner and oven then returned to his seat. "My first worry was getting her car away from here and securing the roads. She has data on three flash drives, proving what she says."

"Can you send them to me now?"

"No." He grabbed a beer and took a swig. "They're password protected and encrypted. As soon as she freshens up and I feed her, I'll get additional details to send you."

Water pounded in the shower.

Clicking sounded on Hank's side. "What's the name of the company she worked for?"

Lucas told him.

"Fuck. They're huge and powerful."

What else? Only a mega corporation would have enough balls and arrogance to kill an employee without worrying about the authorities caring. As a teen, he'd read how the Mafia ran roughshod on this country during Prohibition. They had nothing on what the corporate class had done these last decades. Fuck, Ivy League guys in thousand-dollar suits had cornered the market on greed and cruelty. "We have to stop them. Our men and women are at risk."

"I hear you. Did she go to the press yet?"

He guzzled his beer. "She was considering it when the threats against her escalated."

"Phone? Text? Email?"

"All three." He slouched in his chair. "As soon as I can, I'll ask her to bring the emails up, which I'll send to you as evidence. I'll try to get the texts, too."

"Voicemails would also help."

"I can't promise, but I'll try." He pushed his beer aside. "How serious do you think this will get?"

"Very. My guess is the government contract for these meds is huge. No public company wants to lose that much market share. The Street will destroy them. Once stocks plunge, proverbial heads will roll."

He'd pay to see that. "Think prison's also in the future?"

"I wish, but we know how the world works."

It had happened too often. Company CEOs and higher ups claimed ignorance of what happened at their beloved and trustworthy companies. They selected a scapegoat, generally someone with little power in the organization, and pinned everything on him. Or her.

Shit. "We can't let Kenzie take the fall for this."

"Agreed. We'll do everything in our power to protect her. You know that."

He did, but wanted nothing less than one-hundred-percent certainty. Those in Brotherhood Protectors were fearless fighters, but they were too few against a mammoth corporation and the government. If the feds were also in on this as Kenzie said, shit could go sideways fast. "When the guys are researching NSP, have them check into political donations for Congress and lobbying. The FDA too. Whatever ties into the corporation."

"Already on my list. We'll beat this. Enjoy Kenzie."

He pushed back his chair. "Excuse me?"

"Don't play dumb, Rome. I heard how you sounded when you spoke to her." Hank clucked his tongue. "You're a goner already and it's certainly time. If the rest of us have settled down, you should too."

There was no way Lucas could comment on that without digging himself deeper. Sure, he liked Kenzie. What man wouldn't? She was great to look at, sharp as fuck, and fun—when she wasn't trying to run things. Even during those times, he cut her more slack than he had any other woman.

"Hey, you still there?" Rapping noises sounded on Hank's end. "Or are you and Kenzie taking a moment for yourselves?"

"Want to ask her?"

Dead silence.

No guy like being put on the spot, Hank included. "What else do you need from me?"

"Let me go down the list."

They brainstormed for several minutes before ending the call. The monitors showed nothing untoward on the property, not even a bobcat or cougar stalking the grounds, despite them being nocturnal. Given his presence here, they generally stayed away, though it wasn't unknown for hungry animals to cross territories and take risks. If one had happened upon her when she'd been stumbling around…

No. He didn't want to imagine anything awful. What she already faced was bad enough.

The water still ran in the bath, giving him a chance to deliver the clothes he promised. He dropped several flannel shirts on the mattress, not knowing which colors she'd like best. Another pair of socks followed. His spare jeans would swallow her, but his Ranger sweatpants could work.

Finished, he padded down the hall as quietly as he could. The shower shut off. Rather than using the stove and oven to finish dinner, he nuked everything.

Her sighs then a moan floated down the hall.

If he had to guess, he'd say she struggled to get the sweatpants to fit her much smaller bod. *Damn.* He should have put out a belt or a rope for her to use around her waist. *Later.* While she ate. During the remaining evening, he expected her to relax and enjoy her stay as he did the work.

Another consideration he'd never shown another woman. He wasn't a dictator by any means, his manners spot-on when it came to females. However, serving them as if he were the help rather than an equal had never crossed his mind.

She's scared. There's a hit out on her.

Only a prick would expect her to prepare her own meal under those circumstances. He was merely being a gentleman, as his parents had taught him and the military had further pounded into his skull.

Her footfalls sounded and were coming his way.

She rounded the corner and pointed. "Do. Not. Laugh."

Fuck. That was like asking him to stop

breathing. "Sorry." He covered his mouth, but his shoulders shook. "You look good."

"Bull." She'd tied the sweatpants waist into a knot that rested inches beneath her boobs. His red-and-yellow checked shirt fell below her knees in back. She'd rolled the sleeves up numerous times. They still hung over her fingers.

He rubbed his chin. "Looks like the water shrunk you."

"Or you're too big."

"You like your men small?"

She stopped folding over the right cuff, her gaze darting to his fly, her cheeks turning as red as the shirt.

Waiting for her response—hell, encouraging it—wasn't playing fair, but at this point, he was ready to ditch the games. Heaven couldn't have smelled better than she did. His throat tightened at her flushed face and silky neck. The color looked damn good next to her hair, those locks finger-combed and mussed, as they would be after she enjoyed an evening in bed.

With me.

Sex wasn't love. Hungering for her was

totally understandable. Nothing to worry about.

Except it wasn't happening.

She'd already padded past him and sniffed. "Smells great."

"What happened to your glasses?"

She touched her face. "I left them on your dresser. I only need them to drive in the dark. Sit." She pointed at his chair. "I'll have your dinner on the table in a sec."

"My table. My food. My house. My rules." Hands on her shoulders, he directed her to the next chair. "Once you're down, don't move."

Seated, she wound a tress around her finger. "Why not?"

He ladled stew into a bowl. "I figure if you're standing and not holding onto my sweatpants, they'll fall around your ankles." He delivered her dinner and pushed the warmed biscuits closer. "Since I forgot to put out my underwear for you... Want me to finish that thought?"

"What do you think?" She dug into the stew, stopped chewing, and stared.

"What? You hit a bone? It's too hot? Too cold?"

"Try freaking delicious." She gobbled it as Bullet did his meals even though he'd never gone hungry. Kenzie had. The moment she lowered her spoon, Lucas refilled her bowl, put the pot on the table, and sat. "Eat all you want. There's enough here for thirds, fourths, and beyond."

"Thanks." She finished several mouthfuls before her chews slowed. "Don't tell me you actually cooked this."

"Okay, I won't. Except I did."

"Get out." She pushed his shoulder. "This is…" Her glee faded to apprehension.

Why? The monitors showing the outside were empty except for what should be there. "What?"

She licked juice off her lips. "I was going to say the stew's awesome, but— What exactly is in here?" She made a face and leaned away. "Did you kill it?"

Keeping in his laughter wasn't easy. "No. I don't have any cows on the property. Plus, I get my meat in a supermarket, the same as nearly everyone else. I'm former military, not Robinson Crusoe."

"Got it." She dumped more into her bowl then swore. "I'm not leaving you any."

"I already ate. Go on, finish everything."

"No can do. Get your bowl."

Once he had, she filled it and pushed four biscuits to his side. "Butter?"

"Coming up. Along with your hot chocolate." Which he'd prepared as she showered.

She clapped then stopped. "Marshmallows?"

He let out a deliberately long and noisy sigh. "Good Lord, woman, you're are fucking hard to—"

"Nope, I'm good. Sit." She patted his seat. "Did your mother or the Army teach you how to cook?"

"Mom." He broke several biscuits in two and slathered real butter on them. "Since she had all boys, she needed help in the kitchen. We were it."

Kenzie swiped a biscuit he'd prepared, took a huge bite, and moaned. "God, that's amazing."

Crumbs and butter clung to her mouth, inviting him to suck it clean. Keeping his head, he handed her a napkin.

"Thanks." She tongued her lips instead. "How many brothers do you have?"

"Two. Both older."

She nodded, took another bite, and chased it with hot chocolate. "They're Rangers and snipers, too?"

"God no. Frankie's a software engineer like Dad. They work at the same company. Sam's an educator like Mom. She does elementary. He teaches high school math."

"Great professions. What's with the 'god no' about them being military?" She pointed her spoon at him. "Didn't you like what you did?"

"My parents didn't. When I enlisted, they gave me no end of grief. Dad wanted me to be a doctor. Mom would have been happy if I'd become an oral surgeon."

Kenzie took in him and frowned. "Nope. I can't see you as either. Ranger fits you perfectly."

"Yeah?" His already high confidence soared. Before he got too giddy and crossed any lines, he calmed. "I should have you talk to them."

"They're still not happy about your career choices?"

He prepared two more biscuits and put

them on her plate. "They'd like me to choose an occupation where danger's never on the horizon."

"Like mine?" She slumped then shook her head and tapped her spoon against his plate. "How'd you manage to save enough dough to buy this place? Are you in debt up to your eyeballs? Will what I pay you for protection help?"

Before she offered to retire his debts, if she could, he fessed up. "I didn't pay a cent for my land or the cabin. I inherited it."

Her mouth fell open. "You had wealthy grandparents? What did your brothers and parents get?"

"Nothing." Finished with his stew, he used a biscuit to sop up the juice. "I got it from a buddy's dad. He was the one who had endless cash."

"Which he willed to you, because...?"

Lucas didn't often talk about himself. Somehow, it felt wrong. Considering how she stared and waited, he didn't have much choice. "I saved his son during combat. It was nothing. Anyone would have done the same. No big deal."

"I bet your buddy and his dad didn't think that." She rested her elbow on the table, her head in her hand. "I'd ask you what happened, but I sense you don't want to talk about it."

"Thanks. I don't." In the last few seconds, the air seemed to get thicker, his ability to breathe more difficult. A woman asking who he saved or lost during his military service was tantamount to her wanting to compare his dick to other guys'. An intimacy he didn't want to get involved in.

She stroked the table near his plate. "Can I ask you something that's not combat related?"

In his experience, any personal question might not be wise. "I won't answer if I don't want to."

"Agreed. What was a rich guy's kid doing in the service? That's not normal."

He barked a laugh, the sound startling Bullet. After gesturing the shepherd back to its place, Lucas sagged in his chair. "Dave's a good guy and one of my best friends. Despite his father's wealth, or maybe because of it, he wanted to serve those who have far less. It was either the Peace Corps or the military."

"Is he still a Ranger?"

"He is." Lucas grabbed another beer and brought the hot chocolate to the table to refill her cup. "Next year he gets out. I'm trying to talk him into joining our team. Enough about me." He sat. "What's your story?"

She blew on her drink then sipped it. "Not much to tell. My parents died in a plane crash when I was seven. Their friends were along, the husband piloting the private aircraft. They flew here from Palo Alto, where I grew up. This resort was my parents' favorite spot to go for a mountain getaway. More so than those in California."

The loss sounded in her voice, her lingering pain killing him. He squeezed her hand. "I'm sorry. If you don't mind me asking, who raised you after that?"

"I had one aunt on my mom's side." She put down her cup. "Brain cancer took her when I was eighteen. At least I was an adult and at Stanford then, so I didn't have to go into foster care."

Maybe not, but she was alone and had been for too long, no blood relations to count on. "That's awful."

She waved away his concern. "I'm used to

being by myself." She regarded her unfinished meal, rather than him. "It's okay."

Bull. The misery on her face didn't lie. First, she'd lost everyone who'd valued her existence then poured her love into work, which betrayed her. No one should have that much bad luck.

He stroked her fingers. "I have no doubt about your capabilities or that you like solitude. Living here, I know where you're coming from. However, you have me now. That's something I want you to believe in and to count on."

She raised her face. Tears sparkled in her eyes. "Hold me? I mean, if you don't mind."

His chest ached at how lost she looked, sorrow gripping him. "Of course, I don't." To deny her this moment wasn't something he could or wanted to do.

He gathered her close, his arms wrapped around her waist.

She snuggled against him, delivering her scent and warmth. "Thanks."

"My pleasure." Rubbing her back, he comforted her as best he could, wanting only the best for her always. "I'm not going anywhere."

"I know. You're a good guy."

As long as she thought so, that was the only thing that mattered.

They remained as they were, the world going unnoticed around them. At least for him, her presence a comfort he'd rarely known or sought but needed now.

She shifted slightly.

He eased his hold. "You okay?"

"Yeah. But if you're not—"

"I am. Don't worry about me."

"I can't help it." She cradled his cheek.

Without thinking, he kissed her palm. The most natural thing to do.

They gazed at each other, his heart pounding. Words escaping him. Time seeming to stand still.

She touched her mouth to his.

CHAPTER 5

KENZIE'S BREATH caught at Lucas's heat and scent, the glorious contradiction between his achingly soft lips and bristly cheeks. The best of all worlds, though not hers. They were untimely strangers, forced together by events far beyond their control. These moments shouldn't be happening. Tomorrow or the next day they'd likely be over.

She didn't care. All that mattered was what happened now, melting against him her only goal. She wreathed her arms around his shoulders, keeping him to her, and opened her mouth to his.

His tongue filled her and explored before she had a chance to do the same to him, his passion urging her to suckle and welcome, arouse and satisfy.

Nothing else was possible. His taste comforted and dazzled, a unique flavor new to her yet somehow known, and certainly required.

Their tongues played. Lips sought. Hands explored.

With her boob cupped in his palm, he fondled her gently then hard, as she liked, his thumb stroking her nipple.

Exquisite pleasure roared through her, the kind that made living worthwhile. Nerve endings fired, sending delight every-freaking-where before settling in her pussy. She couldn't have been wetter, prepared and eager for his cock.

As one, they rose from their chairs, both pressed close, mouths joined.

Somehow, they made it down the hall to his bedroom, not questioning or delaying what they had to enjoy.

He tore the comforter off the bed, his extra clothes scattering around them, one striking the large window.

Immaculate panes recorded her reflection,

the lights in here displaying everything that would soon happen inside, including them naked and rutting like wild animals. She wasn't a prude, but this was exposure she wasn't used to, heat stinging her face.

He caught her discomfort. "What?" He'd already pulled off his sweatshirt and dropped it where he stood, his chest smooth, hard muscles defining his pecs, abs chiseled enough to count each.

Reeling at his masculine beauty, she couldn't think or talk. Dark hairs trickled from his rounded navel to beneath his jeans and the thick ridge behind his fly. Her heart stalled then hammered too hard.

"Kenzie?"

"Huh?"

He rested his hands on his narrow hips. "What are you doing?"

"Nothing."

"I get that." He padded closer. "Why aren't you undressing?"

His voice couldn't have been softer, his features more confused.

Being a guy must rock. They had no qualms about anything. "The window." She gestured to it then the room in general. "It's so bright in here. I know you don't want total darkness, and I don't either, but—"

"Give me a sec." He plucked two flannel shirts off the floor then draped them over the lamps on either side of the bed.

The red and blue colors cast the room in a hazy glow, enough to see and amazingly romantic. Her blood thickened and her heart sang. "You're a freaking genius."

"Leave the praise for later." He pulled a string of condoms from the nightstand drawer and tossed them on the mattress. "Talking, too."

"Yes, sir."

Laughing, they stripped each other, clothes flying everywhere. Both finally naked, they sank to the bed, their mouths hungry and eager, skin caressing skin.

His rigid cock snuggled between her thighs. Her nipples poked his pecs. A carnal world she never wanted to leave.

They rolled from side to side, attempting to get closer, their kisses frantic. Nothing worked. If she could have become part of him, she would have celebrated the notion, needing his warmth and strength surrounding her while also being inside. At last, he rolled to his back and pulled her on top.

She struggled for a full breath.

He eased her hair aside and searched her face, not allowing any emotional distance between them.

With another man, the moment would have proved too intimate and uncomfortable, nothing available to break his quiet scrutiny. She might have cracked a joke or questioned what he was doing. Wasn't possible when it came to Lucas. For him to crave such closeness and to desire her to this extent was the greatest gift he could have offered. One she wouldn't waste.

She drank him in at her leisure, loving his long, dark lashes, the small mole on his temple, the laugh lines fanned around his eyes. A faint scar on his jaw troubled her. She hoped the injury hadn't caused too much pain.

Knowing him, he likely shrugged it off, as he did her compliments.

In her world, few men were as decent or as masculine, his hair-roughened body and hard dick intensifying everything female within her, more than anything had in a long while. Her pussy ached, wanting his cock deep inside. Without his tongue filling her, her mouth felt bereft.

Kissing him deeply, she blindly groped for a rubber.

He beat her to it, separated a packet, and ripped it open.

With surprising grace, he eased her off him to sheath himself.

"No." She grabbed his wrist. "Let me."

A broad smile lit his face, delight dancing in his eyes. "Whatever you want."

There weren't enough words or time to convey what she required. Showing him, she pressed her face to his thick, dark thatch.

God, god, god. His musk enthralled. The short, curly hairs entranced. She couldn't smell or taste him enough.

"Hey." He gripped her shoulders. "This wasn't the plan."

"Sorry." She wasn't and took his cock into her mouth.

He gasped.

She sucked him deep, every luscious inch— easily nine or more—until her nose touched his hairy groin. Smelling him came naturally.

Enjoying him the only thing she could do. Her ears buzzed, and her skin burned. There wasn't a better place on Earth than being here, nor anything that could match his balls. Cupping them lovingly, she gloried in their weight and heat, the short hairs furring them. Totally decadent. As male as anything could get.

His groans and panting filled the room.

Wasn't enough.

She released his dick and tongued his right ball between her lips.

An oath tore from him. "No, no, *fuck no.*"

He pushed her back and used his weight to trap her. "That's not happening yet." He caught a breath and swallowed. "Where's the rubber?"

Having held on to the thing, she lifted it.

"Hand it over." Before she could, he plucked it and sheathed himself.

She caressed his balls.

Teeth gritted, he raised his face to the ceiling, his neck corded. "Don't. I mean it." He looked at her, panic in his eyes. "Unless you want me to come while you're way over there and I'm way over here."

"Nope." She released his nuts. "I'm not crazy."

"Good to know." Heaving air, he settled between her legs, his crown touching her cleft.

Fill me. Please.

On one deep thrust, he entered her fully.

Her heart snagged on a beat then pounded wildly, his girth and length stretching her to accommodate him.

Not yet through, he pumped to go deeper, their curls touching.

He pulled in a breath and grinned.

She did, too, then cupped his face to bring his mouth down to hers, the wait for his lips and tongue far too long. *I like you so damn much. I shouldn't, but I can't help it.* With her defenses destroyed and her heart open, she gave herself fully to him.

HAVING KENZIE'S TIGHT, hot cunt sheltering his cock and her tongue filling his mouth was paradise Lucas hadn't believed possible. One he'd honor. No way would he rush this despite his dick already feeling bruised and abused, well past needing relief. His balls were as bad, tightened to the point they hurt.

Get used to it.

He owed her far more than a simple fuck. Only an act of love would do for such a remarkable woman...astonishing moments for her—and him—to savor.

Pumping slowly, he suckled her tongue deeper, loving her clean breath and flavor, a hint of chocolate remaining. He dispatched it quickly, wanting nothing except the woman she was.

A bright, funny, bossy, and giving person he hadn't believed existed before tonight. One he feared he'd never find again once she left.

Despair gripped him when it shouldn't. He'd never been the romantic type, not even during middle school when his hormones kicked in worse than if he'd mainlined steroids. Moping over a particular girl hadn't been his thing. If any didn't want him, he moved on and pitied the guys who couldn't let go and suffered.

Getting close enough to Kenzie, physically, didn't seem possible. Despite his numerous tries and the scant distance between them— barely enough to allow a full breath—it was still too much.

He thrust harder and pumped faster.

She gripped his biceps, not to push him back but to pull him nearer.

That's my baby.

Wait. What?

She wasn't his. Couldn't be. She had a life and career outside these mountains. He didn't want city life ever, except when he had to endure it during an assignment or when he was on a date.

They hadn't come close to doing that. Hell, they'd just met. What they'd learned about each other thus far amounted to less than zip.

He felt as if he'd known her forever. She made him that comfortable. Even when she ignored his suggestions so she could run things.

What's happening to me? Uncertain, he battled her tongue, intent on winning, and finally pushed his inside her mouth.

She squeezed her cunt hard and fast around his cock.

Pleasure shot to his eyes then down to his ankles, leaving him breathless and weak. *Shit.* Extra stimulation wasn't what he needed. Getting her to stop unlikely.

Maybe that was why he craved her to the

extent he did. She was his equal in every way, except for his strength.

Tempering his, he nevertheless pumped more forcefully, quicker, too, and then rubbed her clit.

She bucked, her moans muffled by his tongue. Better still, she forgot to squeeze his dick.

Now I have you. There wasn't a chance in hell she'd orchestrate their lovemaking.

Alternating between slow and fast, he coordinated his thrusts into her pussy and his strokes on her nub.

New moans and a grunt rushed from her. She writhed and dug her nails into his arms.

Flaying him to bone wouldn't keep him from doing this. At this point, nothing would except her telling him to stop.

She didn't, and he kept at it, giving her his best.

Squeals and whimpers escaped her, her cunt pulsing around his cock, signaling her release.

Thank god. He preferred dragging this out until morning, but couldn't, knowing his limits.

Despite gasping around his tongue, she managed to squeeze his cock again, harder and quicker than earlier.

Fuck no—stop!

She didn't and cupped his balls.

The top of his head nearly blew off. His gums tingled, and his shoulders burned.

Unknowing or indifferent to his suffering, she worked him without pause.

Not about to let her beat him at this, he called on all the discipline he owned. Resolve that saw him through combat and its aftermath, keeping him and his buddies alive. Determination nothing would break. Not even a woman he admired and hungered for.

He rubbed her clit, making certain to vary his pace to keep her off guard, stopping now and again so she wouldn't know what to expect. All while thrusting his dick into her slowly then fast, taking command.

A squeal erupted from her, her pussy going nuts around his dick. Another climax.

Proud as fuck at what he'd done, he drilled her as if there was no tomorrow, giving her a ride she'd never forget.

She pulled her mouth free and gasped then

squeezed his cock hard and long, holding tight, exponentially increasing the friction between them on each pump.

His hair stood on end. He shuddered and couldn't stop, his nuts and dick wanting him to come, come, come.

No. Damn her. She refused to behave.

He reclaimed her mouth and worked her clit.

She wiggled.

Too damn bad. In this bed, he was the fucking boss.

Just like that, she relaxed her pussy, letting him do his thing.

Not trusting it, he slowed.

To say she played dead was an understatement. Few things were as limp.

Refusing to believe her act, he settled her calves on his shoulders, giving him greater access to her cunt.

Her breathing quickened. Her pussy constricted. Fast this time. No, quicker than that, a damn blur, catching him unaware and sending him sailing.

Fighting release, he plowed into her for all he was worth, shaking the mattress, making the bedframe squeak, and the legs tap the floor.

Despite his efforts, she hung on and aroused him as no one else had.

Together, they reached climax. She ended their frenzied kiss and cried out.

He couldn't make a sound.

She'd stolen his breath, willpower, and what little strength he had left, sending him on a journey he never wanted to end. He spun, soared, then floated higher than the atmosphere, clear to where the universe stopped, his ears ringing, skin so sensitive one stroke on his balls would bring him to tears. Thankfully, she gripped his arms, not his nuts.

Gradually, the feelings subsided, Earth calling him back. He refused to listen or return. This was too nice.

His pooped bod didn't agree.

Trembling, he collapsed, catching himself before he crushed her, his elbows supporting his weight.

She eased back his hair and kissed his cheek. "Thanks."

"Hell, thank *you*." He ground his groin against her pussy, not wanting any separation between them. "For a minute there, I swear I saw a tunnel and, at the end, a bright light."

Her deep laughter knocked her boobs into his pecs.

Having her happy and relaxed was a better reward than any he'd received. If he could have kept her like this always, he would have. However, teasing her was his next favorite pastime. "Given your snickering, I take it you didn't come close to death like I did?"

"Hell no." She cupped his face, her thumbs stroking his cheeks, lids heavy. "I actually crossed over and came back. What's your excuse?"

Trying to beat her at anything wouldn't happen, and he didn't mind. "Someone had to stay here to welcome you back." He flexed his weary dick within her pussy.

She beamed and squeezed her cunt around him. "Good answer."

He thought so. "Am I too heavy?"

"Not at all, but your arms are shaking something awful."

They were, and he couldn't stop them. "I'll be good to go again in a few secs."

"Awesome. One... Two... Three..."

She would count them. "Make that a minute or two." He managed enough strength to lift one hand and cover her mouth. "No need to tick them off."

"Agreed." She licked his palm then kissed it.

Fuck, I like how you play.

His fatigue wasn't as impressed, sleep tugging at his lids. "Maybe I should lie to your side."

Once there, he admired her beauty—ripe boobs, lush hips, creamy skin unmarred by freckles or any imperfections, a curly bush slightly darker than her other hair, its color matching her sweet nipples. "Sleep with me?"

For some reason, he didn't want to do so alone.

"Oh yeah." She rested her palm on his chest.

He caressed her hip, his leg over hers. "Comfortable?"

"Uh-huh."

Their breaths collided, and their eyes closed. Darkness and peace surrounded them.

CHAPTER 6

THE FOLLOWING MORNING, Kenzie woke before
Lucas. His firm ass, epic dick, amazing balls,
and everything else on him held her full attention. Sadly, reality intruded, breaking it.

First, she scrubbed her socks in the kitchen
sink to avoid waking him then tended her
muddy jeans. Too late, she realized there
wasn't a dryer in here. Maybe behind the other
bathroom door she'd noticed, except the noise
in there would easily bother him. Wearing wet
clothes wasn't pleasant, but fighting to keep his
sweatpants up and his shirt sleeves from falling
over her hands had its own drawbacks.

She could always go nude but wasn't ready
to strut past the countless windows in here

despite what they'd enjoyed last night. Given her rotten luck, Hank's people might show up unexpectedly.

Cringing at the thought, she fed Bullet and would have done the same for Caesar, except she wasn't certain what he ate. For her and Lucas, she rummaged through the cabinets and fridge to see what he'd stocked.

By the time she had bacon frying, new biscuits baking, and the table set, he strolled into the room, naked as the day he'd been born.

He yawned and stretched.

She drooped against the stove, her legs too weak to keep her up. The dark hair in his pits added to his already colossal virility. Even flaccid, his cock was one breathtaking sight, the shaft thick and long, his crown plump and smooth, its color as ruddy as his small nipples. When it came to his balls... Her insides hurt she wanted them in her mouth so badly.

He smacked his lips, did a double take, then frowned. "You're dressed. Why?"

Pointing out the obvious, she gestured to the windows.

"Good god." He gripped the chair back. "No one's around or will be. Bullet sure as hell doesn't care if you're naked. Caesar doesn't either. I do. Undress. Now."

She arched one eyebrow.

His military behavior morphed into conduct a civilian would like. "Please?"

"What if Hank's guys show up?"

"They'd call first, giving you ample time to put everything back on." He screwed up his mouth. "Surely, you don't think I want other guys seeing you nude."

He wouldn't. That wasn't the man he was. She put the spatula aside. "You should have told me that before I came out here."

His head fell forward. "If you hadn't left me in there sleeping, I would have."

"Point taken." She ditched her clothes and flung out her arms. "Better?"

"Not yet." He was on her in a sec, his kiss deep and wet, but not feverish like last night. His passion lazy and longing, the kind that satisfied but also reached her soul.

Her escalating feelings for him and what they were doing was crazy, but stopping now wasn't possible. She drove her fingers through his tangled hair, keeping him to her.

Pop.

Bacon grease spattered them.

She winced.

He released her immediately and lowered the flame. "I'll finish this. You okay?"

"Not if you expect me to watch you do all the work. I am capable of helping."

"Never said you weren't." He kissed her neck.

His warm breath, soft lips, and stubble were too much to resist. Her legs folded, sending her into him.

He slipped his arm around her waist. "Say the word and I'll turn off the burner and oven. We can use the sofa this time."

They'd have to shoo Bullet from it first. Plus, there were other considerations in the real world, not the X-rated wonderland they currently inhabited. "I should open and download my flash drives."

Disappointment pinched his features, but he shook it off quickly. "That's what I was going to suggest when I offered to finish breakfast—before you accused me of questioning your abilities."

"My bad." She powered up his computer. "Password?"

"Studley Doright."

She laughed so hard she bent at the waist, hands on her knees. "It is not."

"You're sure?"

Not any longer. She keyed in what he'd said. The homepage popped up. "Wow. I thought you'd have something intricate like military codes or something."

"They're classified."

She wasn't certain if he was pulling her leg or not.

He flipped the bacon. "Before you open your drives, get into your email account. Hank needs the threatening ones you got, plus your texts, and the voicemails."

She chewed her lip.

His rich skin lost too much color. "Please, tell me you didn't delete everything."

"I didn't. I knew I might need them for later when I sue those bastards from here to eternity." She sat. "My smartphone's in my car. I take it Hank's guys have already towed it away?"

"They better have."

He brought up the outside cameras. The area where her car had been was empty, the ground returned to its natural state, no tire tracks or depressions. "I'm sure he has your phone. Give him the password and he'll download everything for you."

Not everything. "The goons who called left their messages on my home phone. It's a landline like yours."

"No problem. We can download them to my computer." He poised his hands above the keyboard. "I'll show you how."

"If they're still there." She rubbed her temple. "If they had a key or whatever to get inside my place to plant tracking devices, once I left for good I'm sure they returned to erase the messages. Right?"

He drummed the table. "Only one way to find out. Do you know how to collect your voicemails from another phone?"

"Learned that before I knew how to walk."

He kissed the top of her head. "Like I said, smarter than hell."

His praise buoyed her spirits. The empty voicemail at home killed her joy. "They're gone."

"No biggie." He hugged her. "We'll have you emails and texts."

"Unless they got into them, too." Hurriedly,

she checked Gmail and released her breath, not realizing she'd been holding it. Every rotten threat was there in a hidden folder she'd created. "What's Hank's email?"

Lucas told her and returned to the stove.

She forwarded everything she had then called Hank who opened her smartphone and found the texts.

Elated, she bounced on her chair. "Can you find out who sent them? Preferably a location?"

"Sorry, I can't promise. However, we do have the best forensic computer experts at our disposal. If the addresses are available, they'll get them."

It wasn't the answer she wanted, but was a start.

COPYING her flash drives to Lucas's laptop then shooting them to Hank took longer than Kenzie expected. Lunch passed in a blur. She barely ate despite Lucas's urging.

As the sun lowered, she kept checking her email and waiting for the phone to ring with news concerning the perps' names and addresses.

Nothing.

He massaged her shoulders. "Investigations take time, especially when hunting down professional criminals. Real life isn't like *Law and Order: SVU*."

"I know." She squeezed his hand. "I can't help being anxious. While we're searching for answers, NSP is shipping their poison to every combat area the military's involved in. Someone else is going to get cancer like those soldiers I told you about. Or psychosis and genetic defects. This shit won't only maim people who are already alive but their unborn children. We have to stop them."

He hunkered down at her side. "We will. You have my word. I won't stop until that shit's off the market and those responsible at NSP get serious jail time."

She threw her arms around him. "I can't thank you enough."

"Hell, I haven't done anything yet."

He'd believed her when no one else had, was risking his safety to protect her, and didn't care if the ghouls working for NSP and the government threatened to ruin his life. His only concern was doing the right thing. "You've done more than you can imagine or I have enough years to relate, even if I lived to a hundred. I owe you everything."

"Bull." He caressed her. "I'm not keeping tally. If I were, you'd still owe me squat."

She buried her face in his neck and breathed him in. "Not even a good time in bed? Or on the sofa? Maybe the kitchen ta—"

Before she could finish, he'd hauled her over his shoulder and raced down the hall to their bedroom.

DAYS PASSED with nothing substantial from Hank, and it drove Lucas fucking crazy. There had to be some way to move this along faster.

Think, dammit.

Having Kenzie naked and snuggled close wasn't helping matters. Whenever she was around, his IQ decreased by too many points, the male animal inside him taking over.

Not tonight. He had to do something, but what?

An idea edged close, or rather a name, then floated away.

He willed it back, but it remained elusive.

Something that started with a B? *No.* A D. He thought back to everyone working for Brotherhood Protectors whose first or last names began with that letter.

Didn't help. None had computer savvy to find the psychos who'd sent the texts and emails.

Maybe he was searching for a business name. Several popped into his head, all useless for—

Dave.

The name lingered. Hell, it fucking burned a permanent spot in his brain. *Holy fuck.* Of course Dave. His Ranger buddy.

Lucas scrambled from bed and ran down the hall.

"Hey!" Kenzie called out, "What's wrong?" Her footfalls sounded on the floor. "What happened?"

He powered on his laptop. "I need to Skype Dave."

"Who?"

"My friend whose father willed this place to me." He looked at her. "If you're staying, put on some clothes. No argument. I mean it."

She backed away. "Why are you calling him?"

Because his dad had been a one-percenter with access into the highest and deepest government levels. Using his clout, Lucas and Hank could bypass the usual roadblocks and breeze their way to an answer. "He knows people who have the info we want."

"I'm getting dressed." She raced down the hall and shouted, "Don't start without me!"

By the time she returned, he had Dave's image on the screen, introduced her, and told him what they needed.

A NEW WEEK CRAWLED BY, matters not progressing as quickly as Lucas would have liked though Dave had come through on his promise to help Kenzie and him. They now knew the politicians who'd rammed through the meds at the FDA—for a substantial payoff to them and the top people there—and the other pricks who'd buried evidence as to the pharmaceuticals' toxicity.

Next, Dave promised to round up as many whistleblowers as he could to help shield

Kenzie when she released her data to the public. No matter how Lucas tried to warn her against becoming a target, she refused to back down, even if it meant a lengthy prison term.

He'd move heaven and earth before that happened. Fuck, he'd spirit her out of the country, somehow, to protect her future.

Exhausted and uncertain, she lay on the sofa where they'd last made love, Bullet at her feet, both asleep.

A better picture didn't exist.

Beep.

He jerked at the muffled alarm and pulled his laptop closer. The monitors showed what they should, wind ruffling branches and kicking up dust, vegetation wiggling then going still, shadows inert— *Fuck.*

One shifted. The thermal imaging picking up a heat signature too small for an animal. Not a bear either.

A man.

His heart jumped to his throat. Everything he'd learned urged him to douse the lights in here for an even playing field. Except it wouldn't be. The SOB would notice and might take off, prepared to come back another day, his newest ambush deadlier.

How in the fuck did he get through the guys' perimeters?

Too late to ask. Lucas's first thought was waking Kenzie and getting her to the panic room off the bath. An area he hadn't mentioned, not wanting to frighten her.

He should have.

His options now meant waking her and trusting the motherfucker outside wouldn't notice or take a shot, through bulletproof glass, while she crossed the room, or hoping she'd stay asleep, hidden by the sofa.

During these last days, he'd learned she was dead to the world when she rested. Taking a chance on that, he faked a yawn and a stretch then padded toward the hall. Once he was out of sight, he bolted down it.

In his bedroom, he yanked on his jeans and boots then pulled out three rifles any sniper would be proud to own. He hauled one over each shoulder, held the third, then grabbed his handcuffs and thermal goggles.

Halfway down the hall, Kenzie approached.

She halted, her mouth falling open at his weapons.

Before she could say a word, he clamped his hand over her mouth and spoke as quietly as he could. "Someone's outside. Stay here. I mean it. If you budge an inch or breathe too hard, you could get me killed."

Tears ran down her face, but she nodded.

"Is Bullet still asleep?"

Another nod.

Hopefully, he'd stay that way. If the following moments turned into a battle, the suppressors—also known as silencers—on Lucas's weapons and the assassin's wouldn't disturb the shepherd. In all likelihood, he'd remain safe.

He gave Kenzie the rifle he held. "If anyone comes inside, kill them." He explained how to position and fire the weapon. "Don't think, argue, or beg. Shoot."

"But—"

"Fuck that." He shook her shoulders. "Do as I say. Stay here. Keep the rifle aimed."

Before she could speak, he dashed to the back door and held his breath.

No noise sounded from boots crunching gravel or kicking aside rocks.

Either the intruder was too far away or the wind and rattling branches masked the sounds.

Unable to wait and risk the worst, he stole outside and raced to the nearest shadows. Hidden within them, he slipped on his goggles.

The hired killer inched closer to the cabin and the sole door on that side. He leaned right and left, checking the windows.

Trying to determine movement. The best kill shot.

Not tonight, fucker.

Lucas propped his rifle on his shoulder and squeezed off a shot.

The bullet pinged next to the prick's foot.

He jumped back, his head snapping up.

The red-dot sight from Lucas's rifle shone directly in the SOB's eyes, warning him against further movement. If he breathed too hard, his brains and life would be history.

Lucas shouted, "Drop it and every other weapon. *Now.*"

His rifle, a handgun, and a knife hit the ground.

"On your belly, hands behind your head."

A second command wasn't necessary. Nor was a gun battle like those on TV shows and in films. Docile as a lamb, the assassin chose life—no matter how shitty his became—and waited for Lucas to cuff him.

Questioning would come next. With this prize, Kenzie now had the proof she needed against NSP and those in the government.

It was only a matter of time before their corruption went public and buried them.

EPILOGUE

A YEAR LATER...

KENZIE FINISHED PACKING HER LUGGAGE, Bullet watching her from his spot on the bed.

"This sucks, doesn't it, baby?"

Head on his paws, he whimpered

"Aw, sweetie, don't be sad. Mama's gonna be okay." She hoped. Seated next to him, she scratched behind his ears. His tail wagged.

If only something as simple as a massage could make the bad go away for her, preferably on a permanent basis. She'd fought the powers-that-be for so long, yet each battle ended with the goal farther from reach.

The night Lucas caught Xavier Zelnick, the assassin sent to kill her, the future seemed beyond promising. Especially when he'd admitted everything to save his sorry ass, the details in his confession expected yet horrific.

Since he'd suspected she was close to where the tracking device last placed her, he'd arrived on the property via the creek where Lucas had thrown the instrument. For days, Zelnick searched for her and the best way to approach the cabin without detection.

NSP's CEO Maxwell Swift had sent him as her executioner. Or rather, he'd set the plan into motion, not wanting to ruin his pristine reputation, and had ordered the hit through his proxies. Some were in government. Sadly, there were also a few military personnel.

Lucas didn't want to believe it, but hard data supported the facts. When money and power were involved, everything changed. Rarely for the better.

She excluded his friend Dave in her beliefs.

He'd taken Zelnick's confession to the FBI. The agency investigated NSP, Swift, the board, and those in the government, and military. Public corruption, white-collar, and organized crime their focus. They eventually threw in terrorism, given the threat against her life.

She'd expected 24-hour coverage and major public outrage when news broke about NSP's role in soldiers developing physical or mental ailments, some dying, while others passed on genetic illnesses to their children.

Some in the media—whose relationship with the government was cozy rather than objective— buried the stories in their newspapers' back pages or during low-viewing times on cable. The so-called patriotic stations either downplayed what her research discovered or called it a conspiracy against the government, military, and business, specifically Big Pharma.

During those reports, advertisements for NSP's best-selling products aired.

Too many in the country raged against her rather than NSP, calling for her imprisonment or death, preferably the latter, as a traitor.

Those military men and women who bore lasting effects from toxic meds came to her rescue, led by Lucas, Hank, and others at Brotherhood Protectors.

In the beginning, they were small voices against the insistent shouts of innocence from

Swift's and the others' high-priced criminal attorneys. They and their clients became media darlings. Hosts on numerous shows conducted softball interviews meant to put them in the best light. Again, NSP's advertisements broadcast during those segments.

Their sales skyrocketed.

Internet personalities noticed the con and joined her side, doing the real reporting the others ignored for profit or stock market gains. Strange times though not unknown. During the run-up to the Iraq war, when most news agencies cheerleaded the search for Iraq's weapons of mass destruction, Knight Ridder dug deep for the truth and found it. There were no WMDs, the war unnecessary, too many lives lost on both sides for something that never existed.

Gradually, public sentiment shifted toward that undeniable truth.

Lucas insisted her testimony during Congressional hearings would do the trick for the toxic meds.

Where are you?

He'd promised to be here an hour ago. Together, they'd fly to DC, as they had during the previous hearings. While she took a seat at the witness table, he supported her from the gallery.

She didn't want to testify without him being there. *Oh hell.* If he'd gotten hurt on his latest assignment…

No, no, no. Phone in hand, she punched in Hank's number.

The front door opened. "Hey," Lucas said. "I'm here. Sorry I'm—"

Her fierce caress and kiss stopped him.

He didn't play dead.

Each new separation they endured during his assignments seemed worse than the last. Since the evening he'd stopped Zelnick from murdering her, she hadn't had the desire to return to her previous life or apartment.

Lucas welcomed her into his home, asking her to make it theirs.

She'd gladly accepted.

He finally broke free and pulled in air. "Anything wrong?"

She kissed his neck, ear, and cheek, his scent filling her, his heat the only balm she required. "Besides having to testify again and take shit from those creeps?"

"I wasn't heading there, but sure."

"I'm fine. Except when you didn't show up at the time you promised, I worried something happened to—"

"It didn't. It won't." He pressed his finger to her lips. "My flight was delayed. Traffic sucked. When I realized I'd run late, I called you every five minutes to let you know where I was. I sent texts and emails, too. You never responded."

She'd turned off her phone and the landline to dodge nasty calls. A ritual she indulged in before each hearing. No matter how many times they'd changed their numbers, jerks always found the new ones. "I unplugged the landline and shut off my phone. Sorry."

"S'okay." He pulled her into him, his bear hug keeping her close. "I'm here and we'll catch our flight as planned. In DC, I'll be with you every step of the way."

She cupped his ass. "Only in DC?"

"Get real." He kissed her gently then hard, impassioned and tenderly, every way she desired. Finished, he rested his forehead against hers. "I'm beside you wherever you go. You're my home."

She hugged him, happy tears streaming down her cheeks. "Same here. Always. "

No matter what happened during tomorrow's hearing or the following ones, they'd be together.

And would remain each other's future.

One she cherished.

ABOUT TINA DONAHUE

Tina is an Amazon and international best-selling novelist who writes passionate romance for every taste—"heat with heart"—for traditional publishers and indie. *Booklist, Publisher's Weekly, Romantic Times* and numerous online sites have praised her work. She's won Readers' Choice Awards, was named a finalist in the EPIC competition, received a Book of the Year award, The Golden Nib Award, awards of merit in the RWA Holt Medallion competitions, and second place in the NEC RWA contests. She's featured in the Novel & Short Story Writer's Market. Before penning romances, she worked at a major Hollywood production company in Story Direction.

On a less serious note: She's an admitted and unrepentant chocoholic, brakes for Mexican restaurants, and has been known to moan like Meg Ryan in *When Harry Met Sally* while wolfing down tostadas. She's flown a single-engine airplane (freaking scary), rewired an old house using an 'electricity for dummies' book, and is horribly shy despite the hot romances she writes.

Learn more about Tina and her novels here:

FB Fanpage: https://www.facebook.com/DonahueTina1/
Website/Blog: http://tinadonahuebooks.blogspot.com/
Newsletter: http://tinadonahuebooks.blogspot.com/p/newsletter.html
BookBub: http://bit.ly/2phWWDu
Instagram: https://www.instagram.com/tinadonahuebooks/
Goodreads: http://bit.ly/1wFmIu6
Twitter: http://bit.ly/1ziy4IU
Facebook: http://on.fb.me/1Dl8DHy
Triberr: http://bit.ly/1CE2ec7
Pinterest: http://bit.ly/1yFLeMx
Amazon author page: http://amzn.to/1ChWFkO
TRR: http://bit.ly/1vb7eEc
Sweet 'n Sexy Divas: http://bit.ly/1ChWN3K

facebook.com/DonahueTina1

instagram.com/tinadonahuebooks

BROTHERHOOD PROTECTORS

ORIGINAL SERIES BY ELLE JAMES

Brotherhood Protectors Series

Hot SEAL Hawaiian Nights (SEALs in Paradise)

ABOUT ELLE JAMES

ELLE JAMES also writing as MYLA JACKSON is a *New York Times* and *USA Today* Bestselling author of books including cowboys, intrigues and paranormal adventures that keep her readers on the edges of their seats. With over eighty works in a variety of sub-genres and lengths she has published with Harlequin, Samhain, Ellora's Cave, Kensington, Cleis Press, and Avon. When she's not at her computer, she's traveling, snow skiing, boating, or riding her ATV, dreaming up new stories. Learn more about Elle James at www.ellejames.com

Website | Facebook | Twitter | GoodReads | Newsletter | BookBub | Amazon

Follow Elle!
www.ellejames.com
ellejames@ellejames.com

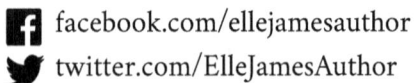
facebook.com/ellejamesauthor
twitter.com/ElleJamesAuthor